Funny Bunnies

MORNING, NOON, AND NIGHT

By Sue DiCicco

Scholastic Inc.

For two funny bunnies, Emma and Jaxon

ISBN 978-0-545-67631-1

12 11 10 9 8 7 6 5 4 3 2 1   15 16 17 18 19 20

Printed in the U.S.A.   40
First Scholastic printing, January 2015

One bunny is up with the sun.

Two bunnies.

Three bunnies.

All the bunnies are up for fun!

Bunnies hear.

Bunnies smell.

Bunnies see.

What is for breakfast?
Pancakes and tea.

Bunnies dress from head to toe.

Ready? Set?

Now here we go!

Bunnies big. Bunnies small.

Bunnies short. Bunnies tall.

How many bunnies do you see?

What a big bunny family!

Pink, orange, purple,
blue, or green.

Together, they make
a great team.

Go, rainbow dance machine!

Bunnies read.

And bunnies write.

Bunnies hop with all their might.

Bunnies lunch.

Bunnies love to play
hide-and-seek.

Some bunnies hide.

Some bunnies peek!

Bunnies up.

Bunnies down.

Bunnies smile.

Bunnies frown.

Bunny cake is easy to make.

Chop three carrots.

Stir.

Pour.

Then bake.

Time for dinner.
Then bunnies can play.

But first they put the dishes away.

Zoom! Wow!
Look out, cow.

Bunny power, now!

Sleepy bunnies.
Time for bed.

Dream a dream
and rest your head.

Tomorrow is another day
to run and sing
and dance and play.